This book belongs to:

_____

_____

For my children,
forever. ~ D.C.

Per Mattia e
Samuele. ~ R.J.

This edition published by Parragon Books Ltd in 2016 and distributed by

Parragon Inc.
440 Park Avenue South, 13th Floor
New York, NY 10016
www.parragon.com

Written by Dawn Casey   Illustrated by Russell Julian
Edited by Laura Baker   Designed by Kathryn Davies
Production by Danielle Nevin

ISBN 978-1-4748-4627-1

Printed in China

The Way I Love You

Parragon

Bath · New York · Cologne · Melbourne · Delhi
Hong Kong · Shenzhen · Singapore

I love you the way the sun rises ...

... this day and every day.

I love you the way the old oak grows ...

... sure and strong.

I love you the way the leaves dance ...

... with dizzy delight.

I love you the way the spring bubbles ...
... flowing and growing.

I love you the way the birds fly ...

... sky-high and soaring.

I love you the way the river runs ...

... light and laughing.

I love you the way the waterfall roars ...

... thunderous and wondrous.

I love you the way the rainbow shines ...

... joyful and jubilant.

I love you the way the clouds drift ...

... drowsy and dreamy.

I love you the way the great mountain stands ...

... unshakable, unquakable!

I love you the way the sun sets ...

... this day and every day.

I love you the way you are ...

... now and forever, with all my wild heart.